Ma Dear's
Aprons

Patricia C. McKissack

Ma Dear's Aprons

illustrations
by
Floyd
Cooper

AN ANNE SCHWARTZ BOOK

Atheneum Books for Young Readers

Remembering Leanna Crossley Bowens,
my great-grandmother
— P. C. M.

For Norma
— F. C.

Atheneum Books for Young Readers
An imprint of Simon & Schuster Children's Publishing Division
1230 Avenue of the Americas
New York, New York 10020
Text copyright © 1997 by Patricia C. McKissack
Illustrations copyright © 1997 by Floyd Cooper
Designed by Ann Bobco
The text of this book is set in Weiss.
The illustrations are rendered in oil wash on board.
Printed in the United States of America
First Edition
10 9 8 7 6 5 4 3 2 1
Library of Congress Cataloging-in-Publication Data
McKissack, Pat.
Ma Dear's aprons / by Patricia C. McKissack ; illustrated by Floyd Cooper.
p.   cm.
"An Anne Schwartz book."
Summary: Young David Earl always knows what day of the week it is,
because his mother, Ma Dear, has a different apron for every day except Sunday.
ISBN 0-689-81051-2
[1. Aprons—Fiction. 2. Mothers and sons—Fiction.]
I. Cooper, Floyd, ill. II. Title.
PZ7.M478693Mad   1997
[Fic]—dc20   94-48450

Author's Note

I recently inherited a plain muslin apron that had belonged to Leanna, my great-grandmother. And although the design is ordinary, the woman who wore it was not. Ma Dear (a short form of mother dear), as Leanna was affectionately called, was a single parent who raised three children in rural Alabama in the early 1900s. She made a living cooking, cleaning, washing, and ironing for other people. These were back-breaking chores, more difficult, of course, because there were no electric irons, washing machines, or other modern appliances. And the pay was very low. My grandmother often told me about her remarkable mother, who worked hard yet always found time for her children and grandchildren—sharing funny stories, teaching them songs, playing games—no matter how tired and sore she was. Those memories inspired me to write this story, in which the real Ma Dear's stories, songs, and games are included.

Here, then, is my tribute to my great-grandmother—and also the countless other domestic workers of her generation. For them the apron was a convenient, all-purpose tool, used to carry wood and kindling, to gather eggs and vegetables, to wipe their brows in the noon-day sun, or just to hide a special treat for a willing helper.

Patricia C. McKissack
St. Louis, Missouri
1997

David Earl always knows what day of the week it is.
He can tell by the clean, snappy-fresh apron Ma Dear
is wearing—a different one for every day.

MONDAY

David Earl knows it's Monday, because Ma Dear puts on her blue apron, the one with the long pocket across the front. It's wash day, and that's where she keeps the clothespins.

First, Ma Dear heats water in the big kettle and pours it into several tubs. Then she rolls up her sleeves and scrubs each piece on her rub board. David Earl would rather blow bubbles, but instead he gathers peach tree leaves for Ma Dear to use in the last rinse.

"That's the secret to my bright wash," Ma Dear explains as they hang out sheets.

At day's end, when the last sweet-smelling piece has been taken off the line and folded, Ma Dear rests in her rocking chair. Her hands are red and chafed. She's so tired, yet she holds out her arms. "Come," she says.

David Earl crawls into his mother's lap. She reaches inside her blue apron pocket and takes out a wooden clothespin. "Once there was a brave soldier . . . ," she begins. The clothespin becomes that soldier standing at attention. ". . . who died fighting out West."

David Earl looks at the flag and sword hanging over the mantel. "His name was Sgt. David Earl Bramlett, Sr.—the same as mine, except I'm a junior," he adds, finishing the story he's heard many times before.

Too soon it's time for bed. Ma Dear kisses her son good night, and he drifts off to sleep, wrapped in a wind-dried sheet that smells of peach blossoms.

TUESDAY

"Why do you always wear your yellow apron on ironing day?" David Earl wants to know.

"Yellow is the color of the sun," Ma Dear answers. "And sunshine makes me feel good, even when I have to iron all day!"

It's Tuesday, and six baskets of clothes sit by the fireplace. Several sizes of irons are being heated over hot coals. David Earl gets to press a few practice pieces.

"No cat faces now," his mother reminds him.

He knows she'll check for any little wrinkles that look like whiskers on the pieces that have been ironed. Remembering how she's taught him, David Earl scoops a handful of water from his bowl and sprinkles it over the fabric. Then he irons, and irons, and irons.

"See? No cat faces," he says, holding up his handiwork.

"Oh my goodness!" Ma Dear replies, laughing at the scorched rag.

The day is long and hot. Ma Dear dips the corner of her apron in cold water and wipes David Earl's face. With the other corner, she wipes her own.

At last, ironing day is over. All the baskets are filled and ready for delivery. David Earl lies fast asleep on a pallet near the door. A night breeze cools the room. Ma Dear covers the boy with her apron and blows out the candle.

WEDNESDAY

After breakfast on Wednesday, Ma Dear ties on her green apron with the hidden pocket. "The treasure pocket," David Earl calls it. The boy helps his mother hitch their wagon to Gracious; they load the baskets, then set off across the railroad tracks to the other side of Avery where all the rich people live.

Ma Dear lets David Earl hold the reins, but Gracious knows the way. His mother rides looking straight ahead, and has told David Earl to do the same. But as they pass, he can't help sneaking a peek at the big chandelier inside the Grandview Opera House.

The mare stops in front of a large mansion on the corner of Main and Tucker Streets. David Earl stands quietly beside Ma Dear at the basement door while Mrs. Hillenbach carefully checks the laundry.

"Your work is good," the woman says flatly, placing a quarter in Ma Dear's hand. Then, casting her eyes down to David Earl, the woman adds, "You may have a peach off my tree if you want one."

The boy stands erect and lifts his head proudly the way Ma Dear says his daddy did. "No, thank you," he answers.

On the way home, Ma Dear makes her usual stop at Hanson's General Store, where she buys a few staples—and one treat.

That evening, after David Earl has finished helping with the dinner dishes, she reaches inside her apron. "Look what I found," she says, pulling a penny peppermint stick from the treasure pocket.

THURSDAY

When the southbound passenger train rumbles through Avery on its way to Huntsville, David Earl knows it's Thursday. And when the sun tops the big spruce like a silver ball, he knows it's noon. Come noon Thursday, Ma Dear puts on a cheerful pink apron, and they go to visit the sick and shut-in.

But first, Ma Dear and David Earl feed the hens and chicks and gather eggs. Then they pick a dozen ripe red tomatoes, some okra, and a couple of cucumbers from their garden. "We're going to take these to Madam Pearlie," Ma Dear says.

David Earl is happy, because Madam Pearlie is so interesting. She was once a famous singer who performed concerts on three continents. All she has left now are her piano, her photo albums, and lots of memories.

"Madam Pearlie, did you really sing for the queen of England?" the boy asks when they get there.

The proud and dignified woman slides to the piano stool. Her fingers know how to find the right keys. "The queen herself requested that I sing a spiritual," she remembers. "They tell me she had tears in her eyes when I finished 'Deep River'."

David Earl imagines he is in a huge concert hall filled with three chandeliers as big as—no, bigger than—the one in the Grandview Opera House. Queen Victoria is seated in her box. Madam Pearlie bows gracefully and begins in a high, clear voice:

> "Deep river, Lord.
> My home is over Jordan.
> Oh, deep river, Lord,
> I want to cross over into campground."

The music stays in David Earl's head the rest of the day. And, that night, just before he falls asleep, he hears Ma Dear humming the same melody as she sews by candlelight.

FRIDAY

"Oh, no, it's Friday again," says David Earl when he sees Ma Dear tie on her brown apron.

"Brown, so it won't show dirt," she explains.

On Fridays, Ma Dear cleans house for the Alexander family over in Mission, about five miles from Avery. David Earl has to go along. "You're too young to stay home by yourself," she says, "so don't even ask."

"Alton Montgomery gets to stay home alone."

"Alton Montgomery is not *my* son."

"But . . ."

"Finish your breakfast, so we can go."

"But . . ."

"No more buts," Ma Dear says in her no-nonsense voice. "And stop whining!"

David Earl eats his oatmeal in silence.

Once they get to the Alexanders', Ma Dear is not so angry anymore. The house is big, but not nearly as grand as the Hillenbach mansion. Ma Dear says the Alexanders are expecting-to-be-rich-people, but they're not rich yet.

Mrs. Alexander leaves a long list of things for Ma Dear to do. While she works, Ma Dear teaches David Earl a new song. "Inch along, inch along like a poor inchworm." She covers his face with a handkerchief. Then she covers her own face with her apron. They beat the rugs, shovel ashes out of the fireplace, and scrub floors.

When they stop for lunch, Ma Dear takes a piece of string from her apron pocket. She makes a Jacob's ladder, a crow's foot, and a cup and saucer. David Earl tries to make the string designs, but they don't come out right.

Back at work, Ma Dear goes upstairs. She changes the beds, dusts, and sweeps every room. Meanwhile, David Earl pretends he's an inchworm as he pulls weeds from Mrs. Alexander's flower garden, slowly moving down each row of blooms.

At sunset, on the way home, David Earl keeps trying to make the string designs. With a little help he makes Jacob's ladder. "I did it!" he says, and does it again and again.

SATURDAY

On Saturday, Ma Dear bakes pies. Wearing her flowered apron, she and David Earl gather apples out back. Ma Dear can peel a whole apple without breaking the skin.

"Throw it over your shoulder," she says, "and it will form the first letter of the name of someone who loves you."

David Earl does, and like magic, the peeling forms the letter J. Ma Dear winks her eye. "See, I told you." Ma Dear's name is Jonelle.

When the pies are all baked and cooled, Gracious pulls Ma Dear and David Earl to the train station, where passengers buy every last one.

At home, Ma Dear puts a coin in a small container on the top shelf of the cabinet. "For your schooling come next year," she says.

Then it's bath time. Ma Dear puts on an over-the-head gray apron. She pours hot water into a round tin tub.

David Earl flaps his arms, splashing water everywhere. "Look, I'm a big fish!"

"You're a big *mess*," Ma Dear says. "Just look at my floor!"

She pours in more hot water and gives him a good scrubbing, from head to toe.

"Are you going to hang me out to dry like a sheet?"

"I should," Ma Dear answers with a gleam in her eye. "But instead," she adds, "I'm going to tickle your toes until you can say:

> Jack wick whack
> Stick ball a smack
> Tick tack mick mack
> Skip scat Jack. . . ."

Between giggles, David Earl tries to repeat the tongue twister, but he can't say it fast enough.

"I give up . . . I give up," he cries, gasping with laughter.

Ma Dear dries him—and herself—with her big gray apron. "Come now, have a slice of apple pie."

SUNDAY

A church bell rings in the distance. That's how
David Earl knows it's Sunday. Ma Dear has a week
of workday aprons—one for every chore. But she
never wears an apron on Sunday.

"This is your no-work-day," says David Earl,
pulling on the pants Ma Dear has made.

Soon as he's put on his one pair of shoes, Ma Dear
brushes his hair. "After service, why don't we take
our supper down to Sutter's Mill Creek?" she says.

"Can I fish?"

"If you fish on Sunday, you'll catch the Devil,"
Ma Dear says, adjusting her hat.

David Earl glances up at the flag and sword over
the mantel and smiles. "Did Pa fish on Sunday?" he
asks as they hurry out the door.